DIARY OF A

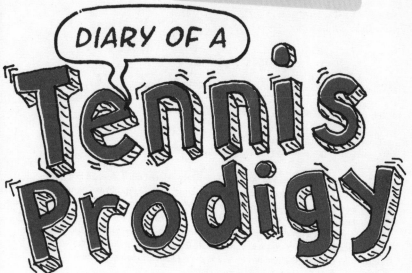
Tennis Prodigy

Shamini Flint

Illustrated by Sally Heinrich

This edition published by Allen & Unwin in 2016

First published in Singapore in 2015 by Sunbear Publishing

Copyright © Text, Shamini Flint 2015
Copyright © Illustrations, Sally Heinrich 2015

Allen & Unwin
83 Alexander Street
Crows Nest NSW 2065
Australia
Phone: (61 2) 8425 0100
Email: info@allenandunwin.com
Web: www.allenandunwin.com

A Cataloguing-in-Publication entry is available
from the National Library of Australia
www.trove.nla.gov.au

ISBN 978 1 76 029 088 7

Text design by Sally Heinrich
Series cover concept by Jaime Harrison
Set in 12/14 pt Comic Sans
This book was printed in November 2015 at McPherson's Printing Group,
76 Nelson St, Maryborough, Victoria 3465, Australia.
www.mcphersonsprinting.com.au

10 9 8 7 6 5 4 3 2 1

MIX
Paper from
responsible sources
FSC® C001695

The paper in this book is FSC® certified.
FSC® promotes environmentally responsible,
socially beneficial and economically viable
management of the world's forests.

MY TENNIS DIARY

I'm in stealth mode.

No one knows where I am.

I'm a shadow, a mystery, a fugitive.

I am also a master
of disguise.

Look at a crowd ...

In a classroom ...

On a beach ...

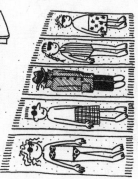

At a bus stop ...

You'll never guess which one I am ...

Who are you? I hear you ask.

Are you a spy?

Are you an alien
in disguise?

Are you on a top secret
mission to save humans
from a zombie invasion?

No you didn't
hear anyone ask-
no one wants
to know.

(The Post-it notes are by
my sister who reads all my
secret diaries without my
permission. She's twelve
going on ANNOYING.)

Be quiet, Gemma.

OI !!!

Actually, I am Marcus Atkinson, aged nine.

I'm an ordinary boy, living an ordinary life, with my father, my mother and two sisters.

So what's the problem?

Why do I hide?

What do I fear?

Why do I run?

I fear my father.

5

I hide from my own Dad.

Can you believe it?

You might think
he's an evil wizard...

Or a mad
scientist...

Or a master criminal...

But he's not.

Actually, Dad is a really nice guy.

He helps old people
cross the road.

He cheers up
crying children.

He gives money
to charity.

And he thinks I'm wonderful ...

So what's the problem?

He doesn't just think
I'm wonderful.

He thinks I'm
wonderful
at SPORT.

And I'm NOT.

What's the opposite of wonderful?

wonder-empty?

I'm wonder-empty at SPORT.

Any SPORT. EVERY SPORT.

How can I possibly know that?

BECAUSE I'VE TRIED...

Anything and everything that can go wrong in SPORT has gone wrong for me ...

But Dad still believes in me ...

The problem is that Dad has written a self-help book called...

PULL YOURSELF
UP BY YOUR OWN
BOOTSTRAPS.

The important thing to know is that
it is not possible to pull yourself up
by your own bootstraps.

I know. I've tried.

It is also not possible to do any of the other things in Dad's book.

How is that even possible?

First you would need a machine to clone yourself.

And Dad doesn't explain in his book how to make one of those...

And why would your cloned self try to stand in your way anyway? If I had a clone machine, I'd make another copy of me, send that one to school while I...

PARTIED!!!!!

But the worst bit in his book is...

Son, you can be anything you want to be! (Chapter 12)

No, Dad, I can't

Yes, son, you can!!!

No, Dad, I can't!!!!

Except I never disagree out loud with Dad.

That's not because I'm afraid that he'll chase me with a broom...

Or lock me in the bathroom until I agree with him...

Or hide my PlayStation on top of a cupboard.

It's because I don't want to disappoint him...

I'm terrified.

More terrified than if I had to fend off a pack of lions...

More terrified than if I had to go on a date with a girl...

More terrified than if I fell into shark-infested waters...

15

19

20

I haven't forgotten the humiliation of that golf kit.

Every single one of my coaches has given up on me.

Never shirk a challenge?

Never?

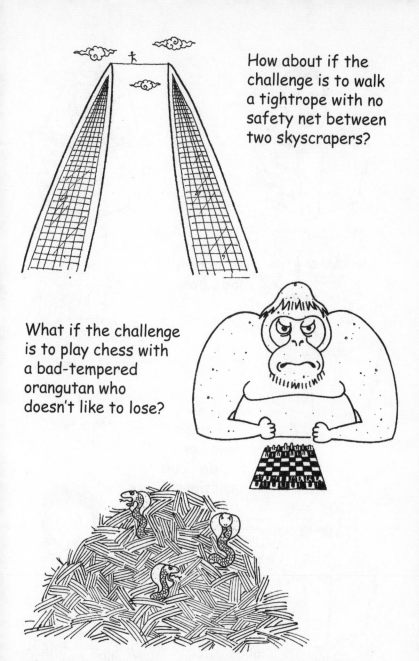

How about if the challenge is to walk a tightrope with no safety net between two skyscrapers?

What if the challenge is to play chess with a bad-tempered orangutan who doesn't like to lose?

What if the challenge is to look for a needle in a haystack that is also home to a family of cobras?

Presidents

Kings

The whole world reads Dad's book...

Queens

Sports Stars

But none of them ever ask the difficult questions...

Celebrities

Ordinary folk

There is no catch?

Is that what the little fish thought before it got eaten by the big fish?

Is that what the big fish thought before it got eaten by the even bigger fish?

Is that what the bigger fish thought just before it got caught by fishermen?

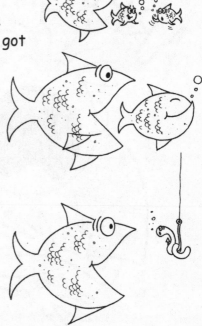

Honey, will you help me with dinner?
Sure, Mum. What are we having?
Fish.
ARRRGHHHHHH!!!!

Nothing annoys me more than
coaches who quote from Dad's book.

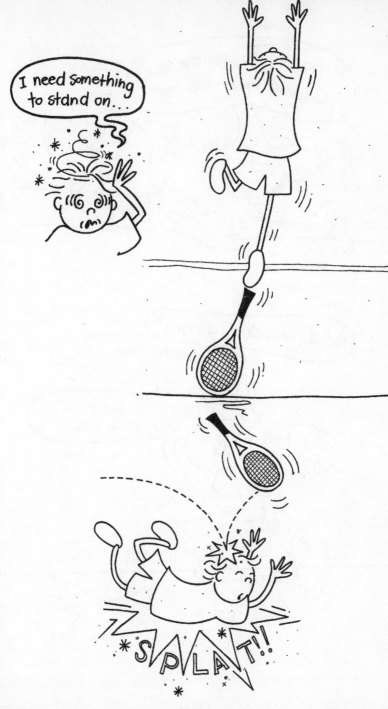

Time to fill in the hole...

TENNIS LESSON NO.2

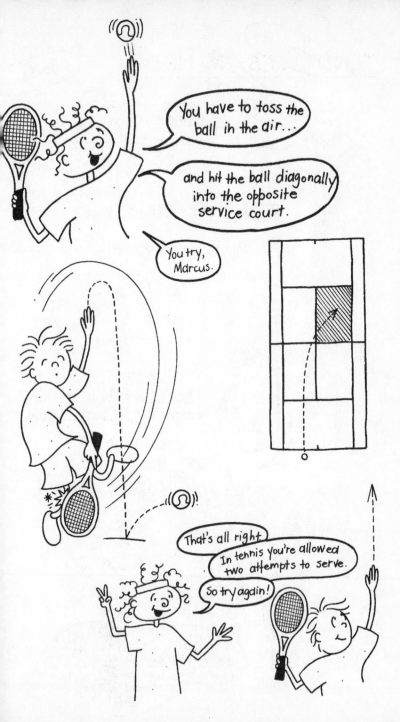

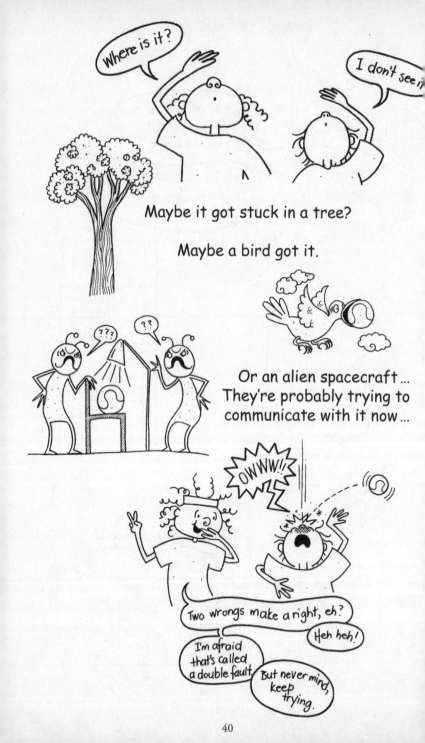

TENNIS LESSON NO. 3

I'd be happy to calculate the amount of spin on a piece of paper – but that would mean I actually have to hit a ball.

*Later Dad told me that a tennis elbow was an injury common to tennis players, to be unseeded means to be a weak player and that Venus Williams is a famous tennis player.

TENNIS LESSON NO. 4

48

49

Dennis the Menace? More like Tennis the Menace!
Tennis the Menace served.
I didn't even see the ball as it whizzed past me.

He served again.
This time the ball
hit me in the stomach.

At least this will be over
soon if he gets 15 points
every time I mess up.

30-0

Tennis the Menace
tossed the ball
in the air like a pro.

This time I saw the ball
because it was aimed directly
between my eyes.

Spot saved me!

54

Tennis the Menace served.

Knowing Spot couldn't help me, I held the racquet in front of my face for protection.

YAY!!! It bounced back over the net.

Tennis the Menace smashed the ball so hard it bounced over my head.

Game!

Phew!!

You see how well you did there son?

I told you tennis was your sport!

I would really love to look at the world through Dad's eyes. It must be quite something...

I bet Dad only sees rainbows without the rain...

I bet birds are singing wherever he looks...

I bet...

...Dad thinks we get along!!

NO!! NOT EVEN DAD COULD BELIEVE THAT!!

What's up with this guy? He beat me at tennis, he didn't introduce me to his sister...

*Later Dad told me that LOVE was what you call a score of zero in tennis.

At the rate I'm going, Harriet will learn to speak before I learn to play tennis...

TENNIS LESSON NO. 5

Even worse than tennis is the conversations between tennis lessons.

He'd just run as fast as he could away from the tennis courts and no one in the whole world would catch him...

TENNIS LESSON NO. 6

What's the best thing about tennis?

Coming home, that's what.
At least at home I know I'm safe.

Safe from the
machines...

Safe from the
coaches...

Safe from Tennis the Menace.

I can play
computer games,

watch television,

do my maths
homework,

play with Harriet

and cook dinner...

I CAN FORGET ABOUT SPORT!!
I CAN FORGET ABOUT TENNIS!!!

Why is there a racquet on the couch?

There's a note.

Pick up the racquet NOW!

I picked up the racquet.

A ball whizzed by my head. I fended it off with the racquet.

It broke Mum's favourite vase.

Another one came at me – I missed and it went through the television.

The next one hit me in a private place. OOF!

And then they were coming thick and fast.
I wielded the racquet like a sword.

I hit some...
I missed some...

Most of the balls hit ME.
And then it was all over...

I looked around. The house was wrecked. Dad jumped out from behind a sofa holding a racquet.

TENNIS LESSON NO. 6

Geez, and James is supposed to be my best friend.
Mind you, he has a point.
Actually, we didn't even get a point.
I stood at the net.

James covered the rest of the court.

James muttered something under his breath.

At this rate, I won't have a single friend left.

80

I looked at Mum.

She slowly winked.

Suddenly,
I understood
what I had to do.

I slowly nodded...

and then I ran to put my new plan into action.

I locked myself in my room and read Volume 1 and Volume 2 of...

PULL YOURSELF UP BY YOUR OWN BOOTSTRAPS.

I skipped dinner.

I skipped tennis training.

I skipped playing with Spot.

I highlighted bits, folded down pages and
memorised sections until I felt I was
ready for anything.

Pull
Yourself up
by your own
BOOTSTRAPS
Volume 1

This match against
Tennis the Menace
was going to be bigger
than...

McEnroe
v.
Connors

Navratilova
v.
Graf

Djokovic
v.
Federer

MATCH DAY

On the day of the match,
I woke up early and made my preparations...

DID I MENTION
I WAS READY?

The sun was shining.

The birds were singing.

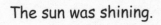

The usual crowd of family and friends trickled in.

The usual crowd of
people hoping to video me
doing something funny
and upload it to YouTube
were there.

Tennis the Menace
was doing stretching
exercises.

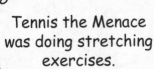

Dad and Coach Ben had
their heads together
in deep conversation.

I walked to the middle of the court.
At first no one noticed and then the crowd grew silent and everyone watched me.

I walked to a section of the court and began to draw and write with chalk on the green surface.

Gemma helped me wheel out carts of delicious canapés I'd made that morning.

Everyone struggled to the front and stuffed their faces... including Dennis.

Especially Dennis since Gemma kept offering him more cake.

Tennis the Menace and I faced off against each other.

Luckily, I had a coin with two heads and another with two tails in my pocket from an old trick box.

I waited at the other end for his serve, shifting my weight from foot to foot, racquet ready.

His first serve hit the net.

OI!!

0-15

His second serve hit
the umpire.

For the next serve,
he threw the ball
so far away, he
couldn't reach it.

0-30

Then he corrected
this by throwing his
ball as high as his
right ear and hitting
himself on the head.

I hadn't had to hit a ball yet.

This time, Tennis the Menace threw the ball straight up, hit it and it landed gently in my court. Even I could put that away. And I did.

0-40

YAY!!!

MARCUS!!!

YOU'RE GOING TO WIN THE SET!!!

But I didn't win the set. I walked up to the umpire.

I decided not to mention the two-headed coin.
There was no need to get carried away.

The perfect sport for a boy and his dog –
especially for a dog as smart as Spot!!

Spot and I raced through the competition.

Spot weaved
through the
poles...

Ran up and
down the
seesaw...

Rushed through the tunnel...

He took all the jumps cleanly ...

I was with him each step of the way, running and shouting instructions.

Spot was perfect!! We were both panting ...

I looked at the clock.

About the Author

Shamini Flint lives in Singapore with her husband and two children. She is an ex-lawyer, ex-lecturer, stay-at-home mum and writer. She loves tennis!

www.shaminiflint.com

Have you read all of my other diaries?